Busy Dizzy

Copyright © 2013 by Dr. Orly Katz

Just to say "Thank you" for purchasing this book,

I want to give you

A gift absolutely 100% free

A Great Creative Coloring Book for your kid

Click here to get your free Coloring Book

www.SimplyMeModel.com/DizzyColoringBook

This story takes place
In a school quite near.
Maybe you know it,
It's not far from here.
The children are laughing,
Here they all come!
There is their teacher,
Her name is Miss Young.

Miss Young

There's David,

Who doesn't look happy today.

And Sophie,

She seems to be feeling quite sad.

The look on Joe's face

Makes me think he is mad!

When Sophie came

Into the classroom today,

She ran to the dolls' house

And started to play.

She knew that today,

She would try not to cry,

so she kissed her mom quickly

and waved her 'goodbye'.

But suddenly Sophie
Thinks she can hear
A strange little voice
Whisper into her ear...

"It's me BiZZZZZZy DiZZZZZZy!"
That voice seems to say.
"You look rather lonely,
Your mom went away!
I'm sure if you cry
Then your teacher will come...
And then you can tell her
You're missing your mom."

The boys are outside,

"Let's all run a race".

David wants to win,

To finish first place!

Then suddenly David

Thinks he can hear

A strange little voice

Whisper into his ear...

"It's me BiZZZzZZy DiZZZZZZy!"
That voice says to him.
"Don't run the race,
There's no way you'll win."

So David decides
That today he won't run.
He watches his friends
And he misses the fun.

Miss Young told a story
And when she was done,
She had lots of questions
To ask everyone.

"Who knows the answer?"
She wanted to know.
Just one hand shot up,
"I know this!" thought Joe.

"It's me Bizzzzzzy Dizzzzzzy!"
He can hear that voice say.
"Put your hand down now Joe!
Quick! Right away!

If you give the wrong answer
They'll ALL laugh at you.
Don't open your mouth,
That's the best thing to do."

So, Joe lowers his hand
And he lowers his head,
Hopes no-one can see
As his cheeks become red.

Then Miss Young smiles,
"I have something to say.

I think Busy Dizzies
Have come here today.

Busy Dizzies are creatures
That no-one can see.

Everyone has them
you know,
Even me!

They sit on your shoulder,
And talk in your ear.
They whisper so softly,
They know you can hear.
They like to cause trouble
And keep themselves busy,
By whispering things
That can make you quite dizzy!

Some make you feel angry,
Some make you feel shy,
Some make you embarrassed
And some make you cry.
Busy Dizzies say words
THAT JUST AREN'T TRUE!
Busy Dizzies make you think
There are things you can't do!"

The kids are amazed,
They look at their teacher,
"Do you mean we ALL have
Our own Dizzy creature?"

"Oh, yes!" says Miss Young,
"And I'll tell you some more.
Some people have one,
Some have two, three or four!"

"Do moms have the Dizzies,
And Dads have them too?"
"My grandma?"
"My grandpa?"
"My friends, John and Sue?"

"All of us have them,
No two are the same.
Each Dizzy is different,
Each one has a name.

"Let's share some stories
Of Dizzies we know.
I think David has one,
And Sophie, and Joe.

I'll bet Sophie's Dizzy
Tells her what to do,
When Sophie wants ice cream,
Or trips to the zoo.

It's called Crying Dizzy,
I bet you know why!"
"I know!" said Sophie,
"It tells me to cry!"

"I have Shy Dizzy,"
Joe raises his hand.
He isn't embarrassed,
"Now I understand!"

"And my Losing Dizzy

Says not to join in.

David is laughing,

"It says I won't win."

"But what do they look like?"

The kids want to know.

"And how can we see them?"

Ask Sophie and Joe.

"Are they big? Are they small?

Do YOU know their size?"

"Nobody knows that!"

Their teacher replies.

"Think of your Dizzy,
I want you to draw it.
What would it look like
If you ever saw it?"

The children start working,
They paint and they glue.
Ben's Dizzy is yellow
And Annie's is blue.

Some of the Dizzies are big,
Some are small,
Soon pictures are hanging
all over the wall.

Joe drew Shy Dizzy,

A very strange fellow.

His teeth stick right out

And one of them is yellow!

Losing Dizzy has lumps
On the end of his nose,
And hair that hangs down
To the tips of his toes.

Crying Dizzy has ears
That fall down to the ground,
The ears are so long
They twist round and around.

"But what should we do
When our Dizzy comes near,
And that strange little voice
Whispers into our ear?"

Miss Young smiled and she said,
"This is what you must do,
If you think that a Dizzy
Is bothering you.

I have a song that you all
Need to know,
When you start to sing it
Those Dizzies will go."

Hey Busy Dizzy!
Get out of my ear!
Hey Busy Dizzy,
You don't belong here!

I think you should know
I don't like what you say,
So GOODBYE Busy Dizzy,
Now JUST GO AWAY!

Hey Busy Dizzy!
Get out of my ear!
Hey Busy Dizzy!
You don't belong here!

I know what I want
And I know what to say,
So GOODBYE Busy Dizzy,
Now JUST GO AWAY!

And so, my dear children,
Our story is done.
We must say goodbye
To our friends and Miss Young.

But if you should ever
Happen to hear
A strange little voice
Whisper into your ear...

Open your mouth
And be ready to say...

So what is MY Busy Dizzy like?

On the following pages there's space just for you,

To name your own Dizzies and color them too.

If you want you can also write them a song,

When your Dizzies wake up, start singing along.

So what is MY Busy Dizzy like?

1. Its name is

_____

2. My other Dizzy is called

_____

3. Maybe I have another Dizzy.
If I do, what is its name?

_____

And what does it look like?

Draw a funny, silly, or ugly picture of each of your Busy Dizzies.

1. Name of Dizzy_____

2. Name of Dizzy_____

2. Name of Dizzy_____

And what about a song?

Write here your own original songs for each of your Busy Dizzies.

Dear Parents,

Welcome to the world of the Dizzies- the negative voices of our children.

Dizzies are strange peculiar creatures, sometimes funny, sometimes mean... that whisper annoying things in our children's ears which prevent them from doing what they really want...

After reading the story you are invited to do the following with your children:

• Identify their own Dizzy and give it a funny/annoying name.

• Share with them your own Dizzies as a child or even as an adult today...

• Draw and create an imaginary Dizzy.

• Sing the Dizzy song (you can change the words to match them to your child's Dizzy).

And don't forget... If you identify additional Dizzies later on (and this will happen!), tell your children that their Dizzy has woken up, and you know the rest...

Lots of luck!

P.S- The tools are also effective for mum and dad's Dizzies...

This book has been created with love and joy
And is very important for me to hear what you
think about it!

Please   press   the   link   below   and   leave
a review.
Your thoughts mean a lot to me.

Please press here to leave a review
www.SimplyMeModel/DizzyReveiw

Other Books by Dr. Orly Katz:

Surviving Primary School

Other Books by Dr. Orly Katz:

Surviving Junior High

About Dr. Orly Katz

Best seller author, Dr. Orly Katz, is an expert for youth empowerment and life skills, who hold a doctorate in Educational Leadership;

She is a sought after guest on TV and radio, and a national speaker and workshop facilitator for parents, educationalists and youth.

Orly is the founder of the "Simply Me" Center for: Leadership, Empowerment and Self Esteem.

Her two book series: Surviving Junior High, and Surviving Primary School, and her yearly Digital course: "Empowering Teachers to Empower Students", are recommended by the Ministry of Education, and are being taught in many schools as part of the curriculum in life skills lessons.Orly lives in Haifa, with her Husband and three children.

Please don't hesitate to contact Orly at any time, at:

www.SimplyMeModel.com